KINGFISHER

THE — YOUNG CHILD'S Busy Book

of
Playing, Learning, Stories, and Rhymes

MARGARET CARTER

ILLUSTRATED BY
MOIRA AND COLIN MACLEAN

Kingfisher Books

NEW YORK

For Jonathan and Helen

Open the treasure chest
Lift up the lid.
Such pleasures are waiting
So do as I bid.

Pictures to please you,
Puzzles to tease you,
So lift the lid wide
And see what's inside . . .

KINGFISHER BOOKS
Grisewood & Dempsey Inc.
95 Madison Avenue
New York, New York 10016

First American Edition 1992

10 9 8 7 6 5 4 3 2 1

Text copyright © Margaret Carter 1991
Illustrations copyright © Colin and Moira Maclean 1991

Library of Congress Cataloging-in-Publication Data
applied for

ISBN 1–85697–822–2

Editor: Vanessa Clarke
Project Editors: Karen Gray and Maggi McCormick
Cover design: The Pinpoint Design Company

Printed in Spain

About this book

I've written this book for children and for grown-ups to share with their children, but every page has a hidden purpose – teaching and learning through enjoyment.

Numbers, letters, shapes, colors – all these are explored through games, stories, and ideas for creative activities. And because a child responds most readily and remembers most easily through rhythm, I've written many of the pages in verse.

I have carefully planned the pages so that you'll find yourself developing and extending the ideas they contain naturally – tailoring them to suit the child you are sharing with. For example, some children will love to join in and imitate the way animals move or the sounds they make; others will enjoy telling the stories in the pictures in their own words. Through asking questions and relating the pictures to their own world, you can help your child make his or her own discoveries about time and the seasons and many other themes.

This is a book that is meant to be dipped into for ideas that suit the moment. Better still, let your child choose the page where you begin. He or she will want to return to their favorite pages again and again. Most of all, have fun together. After all, learning begins with listening and watching and talking – and it's a two-way business.

Margaret Carter

Contents

I See With My Eyes

I see
with my eyes

I smell
with my nose

I touch
with my hands

Voices and sounds

Babies hear before they are born – their mother's heartbeat and, distantly, the sound of voices or music. Newborn babies hear high-pitched sounds more easily than lower notes.

When a monkey hangs
From a banana tree
What do you think
That monkey can see?

He sees the earth
On top of the sky
And trees on their heads –
He wonders why.

He sees animals
Walking upside down
The world is so strange
It makes him frown.

But when he swings
Upright into his tree
It's all back the way
It's intended to be!

I Hear With My Ears

I taste
with my tongue

I hear
with my ears

I speak
with my mouth

Would you like another slice?

Yes please!

Whatever next!
I feel quite vexed!
I've a nose where
My mouth should be.

You see, my dear,
I feel so queer
When I drink
A strong cup of tea!

Who's got my ears?

These ears are far too small.

These ears are too big!

I like these ears, I think I'll keep them.

I can see my ears over there.

"Squeak" Says Mouse

squeak

hiss

moo

meow

baa

quack

too-wit
too-woo

Squeak, hiss,
Meow, moo,
Baa, quack,
Too-wit, too-woo.
Woof, maah,
Buzz, caw,
Neigh, oink,
Growl, ROAR!

buzz

caw

nee-igh

growl

woof

maah

oink

roar

Ollie's Orchestra

This is Ollie. Ollie is an octopus.
Ollie has a tambourine.
Ting, ting, ting-a-ling goes the

Ollie has some castanets.
Click, clack, clickety-clack go the
toot, toot, toot goes the
ting, ting, ting-a-ling goes the

Ollie has a flute.
Toot, toot, toot goes the
ting, ting, ting-a-ling goes the

Ollie has a violin.
Twang, twang, twang goes the
click-clack, clickety-clack go the
toot, toot, toot goes the
ting, ting, ting-a-ling goes the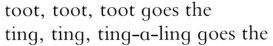

Ollie has a drum.
Boom, boom, boom goes the
twang, twang, twang goes the
click-clack, clickety-clack go the
toot, toot, toot goes the
ting, ting, ting-a-ling goes the

"But now," says Ollie,
"I'm quite worn out!
I've tooted and clacked,
And twanged and whacked,
I've shaken and banged
And made such a din
That my head's in a spin!
Now I need a rest – don't you?"

The Animals' Dance

Make your own musical instruments and dance to songs you know.

Musical instruments to make

◀ Make a whizzer. Clip small triangles from the edge of a cardboard circle. Thread string through two central holes; tie the ends. Hold one loop in each hand, and spin the whizzer to hear it hum – just like a bumblebee!

▲ Make a slither box with some dry sand in a long flat box. Seal the lid with tape and decorate the box. Move the box gently from side to side and hear it hiss!

◀ Old cookie tins or large coffee cans make noisy drums. Different kinds of beaters make different sounds.

The elephant's dance
is grave and slow,
He swings his long trunk
to and fro.
The monkey chatters
in the trees.
The butterfly flutters
in the breeze.
The lion and tiger
waltz paw to paw.
A prettier sight
you never saw.

◄ An old cardboard tube can become a trumpet. Cut the funnel top from a clean plastic bottle. Tape it to one end of the tube and decorate.

► Make a shaker. Put beans, beads, or rice in a small plastic bottle and tape a wooden dowel securely in place.

► Make a tambourine from a paper plate. Thread beads, pasta shapes, or pieces of tinfoil on yarn or string, and tie them across the middle.

▲ Sew bells onto pieces of elastic, and wear them on your ankles or wrists like the lion.

★ *Small objects like beans and beads can be dangerous. Young children could swallow them. Tape boxes and bottles, and thread beads, securely.*

Legs Are For . . .

crawling

toddling   walking   running   hopping

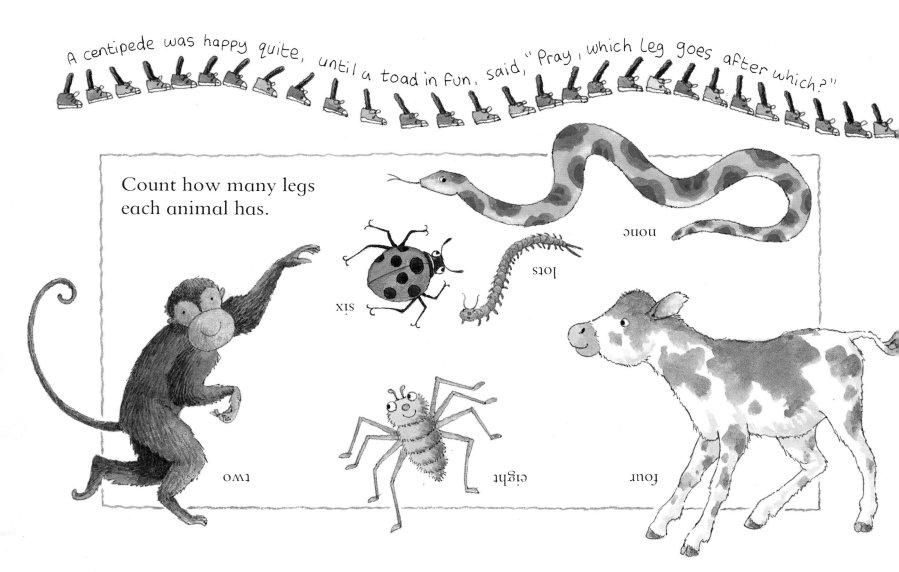

A centipede was happy quite, until a toad in fun, said, "Pray, which leg goes after which?"

Count how many legs each animal has.

lots

six

two   eight   four

jumping   skipping   three-legged racing   wheelbarrow racing

This worked his mind to such a pitch, he lay distracted in a ditch, considering how to run!

All the legs are mixed up!
Can you sort them out?

Prowl Like A Tiger

Can you prowl like a tiger,

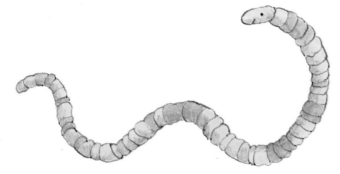

wriggle like a worm,

scamper like a mouse,

flutter like
a butterfly,

creep like
a caterpillar,

or fly like
a bird?

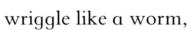

Can you scuttle
like a crab,

bound like
a kangaroo,

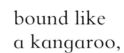

hop like a frog,

or leap like a deer?

stamp like a hen,

Children, you are
very little,
And your bones are
very brittle.
If you would grow
great and stately,
You must learn to
walk sedately!
R. L. Stevenson

All Jump Up

Streetcar Conductor

Pull on the cord
Make the bell sound.
Hold someone's hand
As you step to the ground.

I whirl and I twirl
And I sing as I spin,
The faster I spin,
The louder I sing!
The slower I turn,
The quieter the sound,
And there's no sound at all
If I lie still on the ground.

Painter

Reach up high
Paint to the top.
Wiggle your brush
Slip, slap, slop!

Drummer

Bang, bang, bang your drum
Beat it with a will.
Bang, bang, what a noise
I can hear it still!

Dancing

Try the Animals' Dance on page 12 or Mirror Dancing, where you copy someone else's movements.

Dance like the mirror
Do as I do.
Now change places
And I'll copy you.

Indoor gym

You don't need special equipment to make an obstacle course. Build one with ordinary objects at home. Make sure all the equipment is securely anchored and not too far from the ground.

Step on the stepping stones,
Careful you don't fall!
(They're really only pillows –
Not stepping stones at all.)
Put them in a pattern,
Lay them on the ground,
Then you'll reach the other side
Safe and sound.

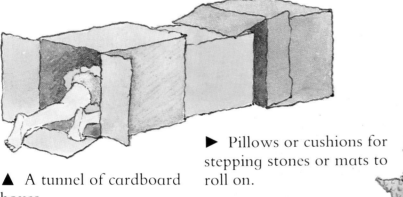

▲ A tunnel of cardboard boxes.

▶ Pillows or cushions for stepping stones or mats to roll on.

▶ A sandpapered, varnished plank of wood with the corners rounded off can be a slide. Support it in the middle to make a seesaw.

▲ A rope, or the plank raised on bricks, makes a good balancing track.

Wouldn't It Be Funny . . .

Wouldn't it be funny
If cows made honey
And all the bees in the world
Said moo?

Wouldn't it be weird
If a worm grew a beard
And a tiger hopped
Like a kangaroo?

Wouldn't it be fun
If an ant weighed a ton
And a hippo
Croaked like a frog?

Then supposing a cat
Could fly like a bat
Or a parrot could bark
Like a dog.
Well, I wouldn't like that.
Would you?

Peter Piper picked a peck
  of pickled peppers
A peck of pickled peppers
  Peter Piper picked;
If Peter Piper picked a peck
  of pickled peppers,
Where's the peck of pickled peppers
  Peter Piper picked?

How much wood
  would a woodchuck chuck
If a woodchuck
  could chuck wood?

I saw Esau
Sitting on a seesaw.

Fuzzy Wuzzy was a bear,
Fuzzy Wuzzy lost his hair.
So Fuzzy Wuzzy wasn't Fuzzy, was he?

Paint, Paint, Paint

Plain or colored scrap paper is fine for painting. Buy powder or poster paint, and see page 92 for recipes to thicken paint.

Mirror painting

Fold a piece of paper in half, and paint blobs of different colors down the crease. Fold again, press firmly and open it out – you've made a butterfly!

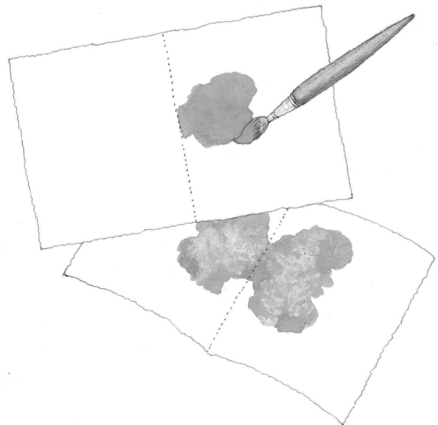

Make a non-spill paint pot

Cut a plastic dish washing detergent bottle in half and cut off the nozzle top. Push the top half upside down inside the bottom half, with the narrow end pointing down. A brush can be pushed through the narrow opening.

Bubble painting

Mix liquid detergent with thin paint in a bowl, and blow gently through a straw until bubbles form. Press a sheet of paper lightly over the bubbles. Or drop a blob of paint on the paper, and blow through the straw so that the paint makes patterns.

★ **This isn't suitable for very young children, who might suck instead of blowing.**

Invisible pictures

Draw a picture with a white wax candle. Paint over it with thin paint, and the picture will appear.

Stencils

Cut a shape out of thin cardboard and paint inside it. Make a doily by folding a piece of paper into four. Cut out shapes and open out; then paint through the holes.

String pictures

Dip a piece of yarn or string in paint; then lay it on paper. Fold the paper over, and slide out the string. Do it again to make more complicated patterns.

Spray painting

Only do this if you have plenty of space and a thick layer of protective newspapers! Dip a toothbrush in paint and spray it on paper by running a finger over the top. Put objects on the paper first and spray around them to make a pattern.

Body Painting

Non-toxic face paints aren't expensive and wash off easily. Try a little on the child's hand first to check he or she isn't allergic to it.

Thick paint is best for body and face prints and, again, check that the child is not allergic to it.

The pictures opposite show the kind of effects you can create using hand, foot, and nose prints.

Boot prints

Fill a tray with paint. Place a "road" of strong paper along the ground. Step into the paint tray and along the paper. The ridges on the soles of rubber galoshes make interesting patterns, or try it with bare feet. A squirt of liquid detergent added to the paint makes it easier to wash off afterward. This activity is best done on a washable floor, or better still, outdoors!

bird

worm

crocodile

fish

Hop on one foot,
Now make a jump.
Walk on tiptoe
Or stamp – clump,
clump, clump.
See what patterns
Your galoshes can
make.
But stay on the paper
For cleanliness sake!

The Color Race

For this game you will first need to make a color spinner or color block – see below. You will also need to find or make a "man" for each player.

Spin the spinner or throw the color block, and move your man to the next square of the color you have thrown. Follow the arrows around the board. The first one to reach the checkered flag is the winner.

Choose your color which will it be?
Red or yellow . . . it's blue for me.
Who will come first?
Wait and see!

Make a spinner

Trace this hexagon shape onto thick cardboard and color each section to match the cars and flags above. Push a sharpened pencil or a toothpick through the middle. Or cover each side of a wooden block with different colored paper, and throw it as you would a die.

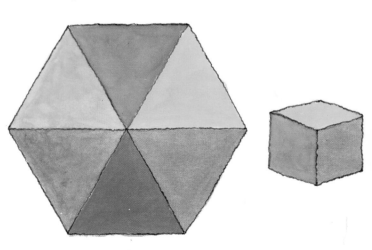

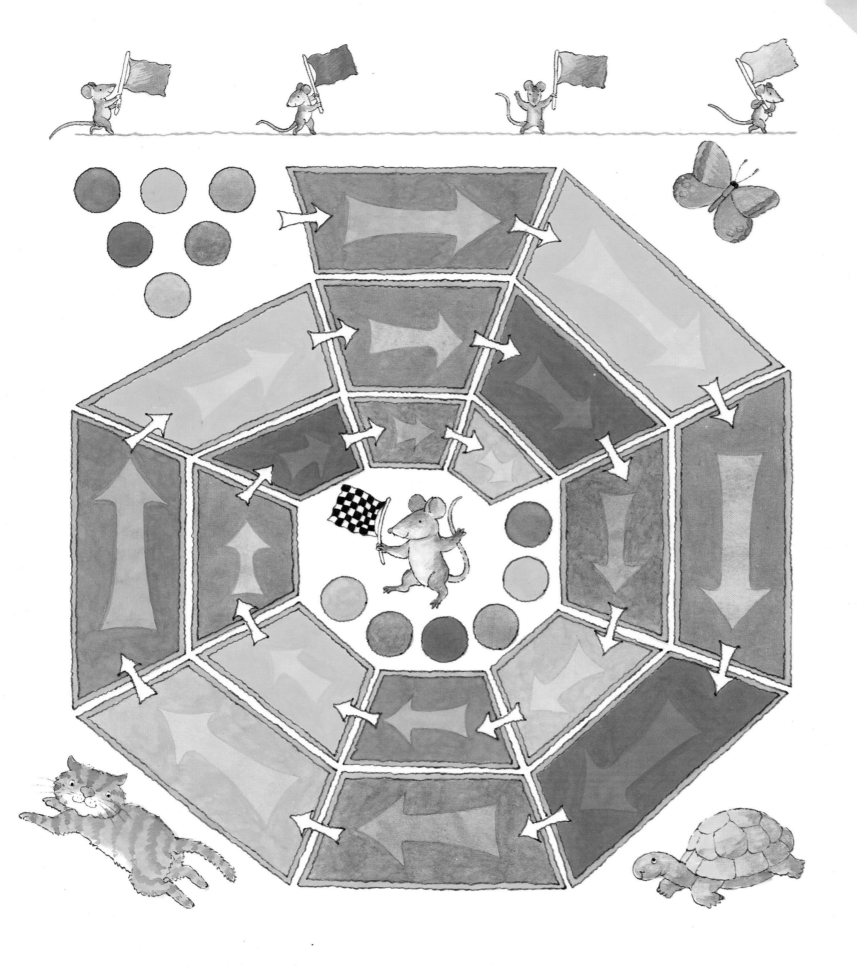

Shapes All Around

Can you see the shapes in Milly Mouse's car?

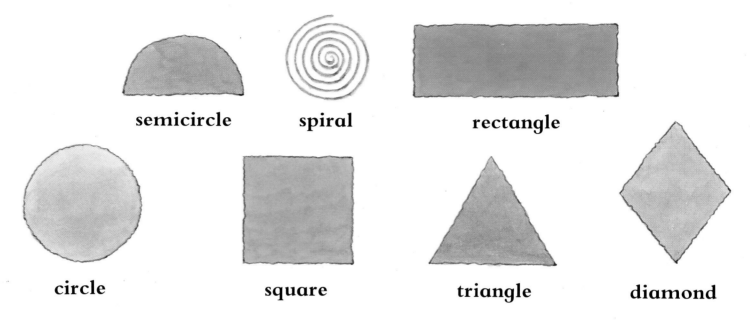

semicircle **spiral** **rectangle**

circle **square** **triangle** **diamond**

How many circles? How many squares?

star

oval

Hanging shapes

Cut colored cardboard into different shapes, and make slits in them as shown.

Join the shapes together at right angles, and fasten with tape.

Hang them from string as decorations or mobiles.

Make larger mobiles from shapes cut from different kinds of paper and hung from a coathanger. Metallic paper will reflect the light. Experiment with spirals and cutouts, too.

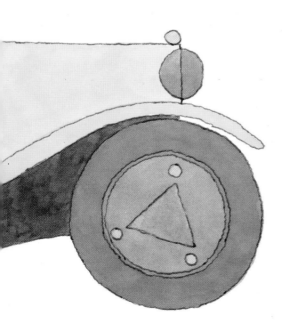

The Story of the Frog Prince

Once upon a time, there lived a princess whose favorite toy was a golden ball. Every day, she would go into the gardens of her father's palace and play with her golden ball. And every day as she played, two big frog eyes would rise up out of the water of the palace well and watch her. But the princess did not know this.

Then one day as the princess stretched out her hands to catch the ball, it slipped through her fingers. Across the grass it bounced and PLOP! into the waters of the deep, deep well it went.

How the princess cried! Tears ran down her cheeks until, through her sobs, she heard a small voice say, "Don't cry, Princess. If I get you back your ball, what will you give me in return?"

And there, looking at her with his big, sad eyes, was a very large frog.

"Oh, anything, anything!" cried the Princess. "Would you like jewels or gold?"

"All I want," said the frog, "is to be your companion. I should like to play with you, to eat with you at your table, and at night to sleep in your bed."

"Oh, I promise, I promise," cried the princess, and the frog immediately dived into the waters of the deep, deep well and, moments later, returned with the golden ball.

But the princess – who secretly thought frogs were nasty, slimy creatures – snatched the ball and ran back as fast as she could to the palace, leaving the poor frog all alone.

That night, as she sat eating her supper, there was the sound of a splish, splash, splosh outside the door, and a small voice said:

"Great King's daughter, open to me.
Remember the promise you gave to me."

"What promise is that?" asked the King, and the princess, very ashamed of herself, told him the story of the lost ball.

"Then you must keep your promise," he said. "The frog must be your companion and eat at the table with you and sleep in your bed at night."

Well, there was no escape. Much as she disliked the wet, green creature, the princess had to share her supper with the frog, and when she went off to bed, the frog hopped along after her, very pleased with himself.

But as soon as the princess was alone with him in her bedroom, where no one could see them, she picked up the frog and threw him across the room. "Do you think I'd let a thing like you sleep in my bed?" she cried.

The frog lay motionless on the floor, watching her with his great sad eyes. And suddenly the princess was full of sorrow. "Oh, frog," she cried, "I'm so sorry – I didn't mean to hurt you." And she picked up the little creature, stroked him, and kissed his poor wet face.

And what happened? Presto! The frog disappeared and in his place stood a handsome prince. "A wicked witch turned me into the shape of a frog," he said. "Only the love of a Princess could free me from the spell."

Well, of course, the princess was astonished – and extremely pleased – and it wasn't long before she agreed to marry him and travel with him to his own land and live with him in his palace.

So the Frog Prince's wish came true after all. He was able to be the princess's dear companion and live with her all his life.

In the Kitchen

Cookies

4 ounces of flour
4 ounces of sugar
2 ounces of butter or margarine
1 tsp. baking powder
1 beaten egg

Cream the butter and the sugar together. Gradually add the beaten egg. Mix in the flour and baking powder and stir into a stiff paste. Add flavoring like chocolate pieces or grated cheese (but omit the sugar if you make these cheese crackers). Roll out on a floured surface, and cut out with cutters. Bake on a cookie sheet at 325°F for about 10 minutes.

Pat-a-cake, pat-a-cake, Baker's man,
Bake me a cake as fast as you can.
Pat it and prick it and mark it with B
And put it in the oven for baby and me.

Face cookies

Pipe cream or chocolate faces onto plain round cookies. Decorate with candy or fruit.

Models

Make models from dough.
See recipes on page 92.

★ *More accidents occur in the kitchen than in any other part of the house. Never leave a child unsupervised.*

Here are some other foods children can help to make:

Milk shakes

Stir or blend mashed soft fruit into milk. A scoop of ice cream makes it creamier.

Flavored yogurt

Mix chopped fruit, nuts, honey, or raisins into plain yogurt.

Sandwiches

Add slices of tomato or cucumber and strips of pepper to make your favorite sandwiches into butterflies or fish.

Or use a cookie cutter to make sandwiches into interesting shapes. Roll a sandwich up, then cut across it into slices to make pinwheels.

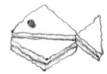

Kitchen experiments

Cut apples into halves and then quarters. Which weighs most? Which weighs least? Fill several glass jars with water and add something different, such as soap powder, sugar, sand, cooking oil, ice cubes, or paint, to each one. Talk about what happens. Does it dissolve? Does it float? Try with hot water, too.

Put an egg in a jar of cold water. It will sink. Take the egg out, and stir two spoonfuls of salt into the water. The egg will now float because the solution is denser.

Growing Things

Seeds

Try sprinkling a handful of fast-growing seeds like, grass or wheat onto damp blotting paper or absorbent cotton kept moist in a dish. Put it in a warm, dark place. The seedlings should appear in a few days. Try sowing the seeds in the shape of your name or initials.

Vegetables

Make a desert island by placing the sliced top of a carrot in a saucer of water. Leaves will sprout in a few days.

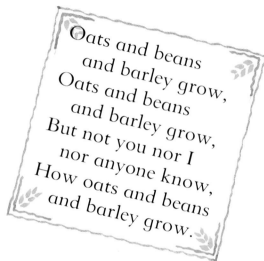

Oats and beans and barley grow,
Oats and beans and barley grow,
But not you nor I nor anyone know,
How oats and beans and barley grow.

Beans and peas

Line a glass jar with damp tissues or blotting paper. Put a few dried beans or peas between the glass and the paper. Fill the jar with water and keep it in a warm place. Watch the roots grow first, and then the shoots. When they are larger, plant them in pots or in the ground.

Plant experiments

Put a stick of celery in a jar of colored water. In a few hours, you will see the color moving up the stem as the celery "drinks" the water.

Try sticking a piece of black paper (perhaps in the shape of a child's initials) on a leaf growing outside in spring. When you take it off after a few weeks, the leaf will be a paler color under the initials where no light has been able to reach.

I planted a seed,
   but nothing grew.
I waited and watched
   and watered it, too.
Just as I thought it
   would never appear,
It popped up a shoot
   to say "I'm here!"

Bulbs

In the fall buy some bulbs and bulb fiber. Put some damp fiber in a bowl, place the bulbs on top, and cover with the rest of the fiber, keeping the bulbs near the surface. Put the bowl in a dark, warm place for about two weeks. When the shoots appear, move the bowl into the light.

Sand

Sand trickles through fingers and oozes around toes. It can be built up and knocked down, made into shapes, or used to bury things. You can buy a sandbox or make one; make sure it is covered when not in use. Avoid anything sharp-edged as sandbox toys. They can be buried and become dangerous.

Use saucepans or colanders as molds for cakes and pies, and shells and stones as decorations.

Plastic buckets make the best castles, and paper on sticks or twigs make flags.

When I was down beside
the sea,
A wooden spade they gave
to me,
To dig the sandy shore.
R. L. Stevenson

and Water

Outdoors in the summer or indoors at bathtime, sponges, funnels, strainers, and colanders all make good water toys. Don't leave children unattended in or near water. There is a bubble recipe on page 92.

Make a waterfall

Makes holes in yogurt cups and string them together from a coathanger. Pour water into the top one and let it trickle down.

Make a dam system

Fill hollows of sand with water and use pipes to connect them.

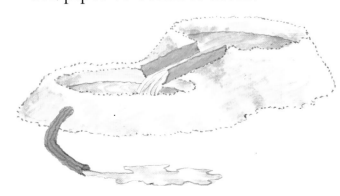

Counting Cats

1

2

Father Cat is far too fat
To fit on this mat.

I think he needs two
Fetch another one, do.

3

4

It seems to me
That he'll need three.

He still needs more
That makes four!

5

6

How *can* he contrive
To stretch across five?

Now what a fix
If we can't find six.

One To Ten

7

"This would be heaven
If I just had seven!"

8

"Please don't be late
With number eight."

9

"I mustn't whine
But I could do with nine."

Although he's fat
This cat can have
Only *one* mat!

10

Did you ever know when
A cat stretched to *ten*?

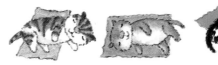

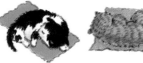

One Fire Engine

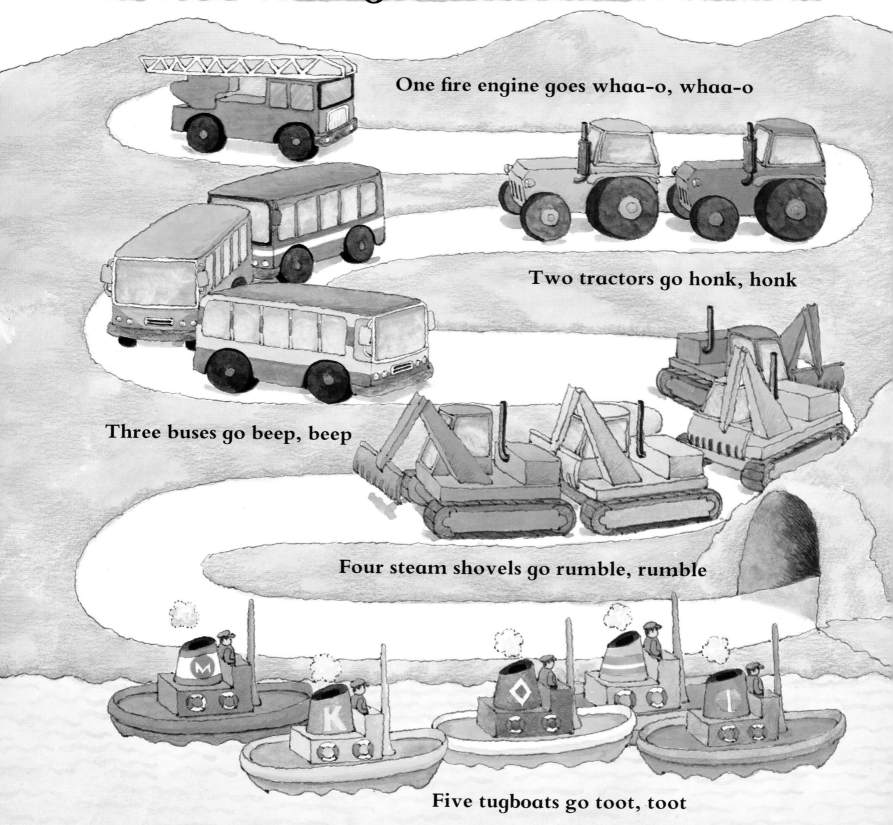

One fire engine goes whaa-o, whaa-o

Two tractors go honk, honk

Three buses go beep, beep

Four steam shovels go rumble, rumble

Five tugboats go toot, toot

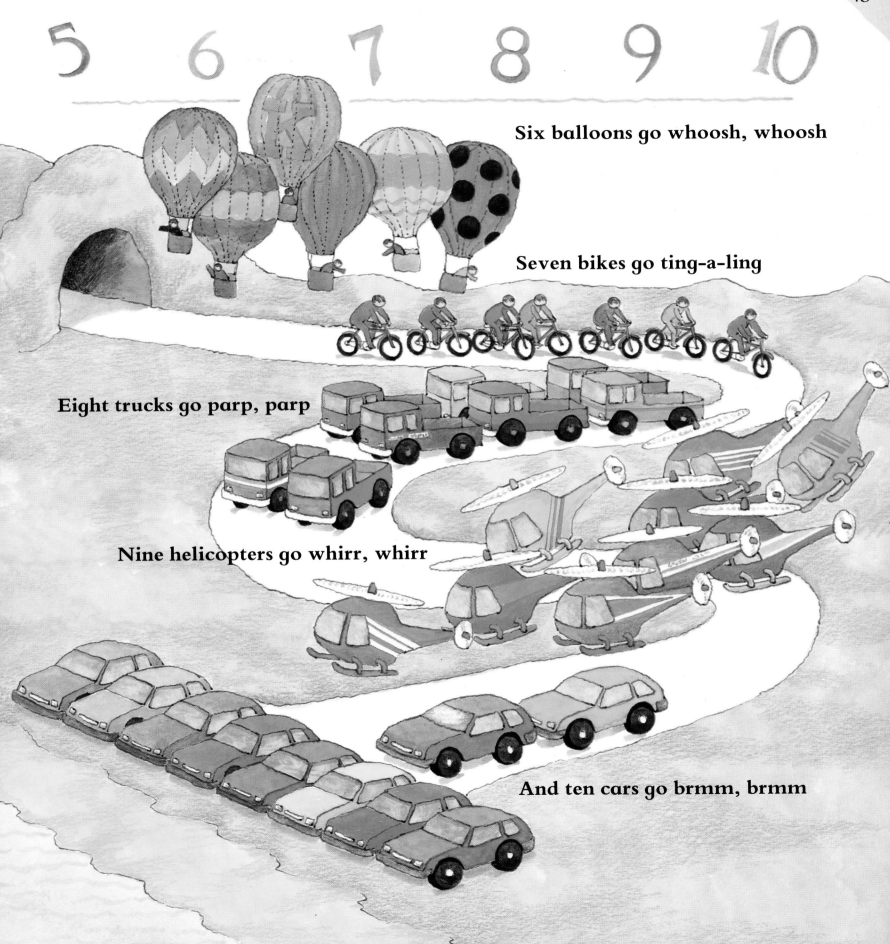

5 6 7 8 9 10

Six balloons go whoosh, whoosh

Seven bikes go ting-a-ling

Eight trucks go parp, parp

Nine helicopters go whirr, whirr

And ten cars go brmm, brmm

A Counting Game

Tinker

Tailor

Fisherwoman

Lady

Baby

How to play

You'll need a "man" for each player and a die. Take turns to throw the die and move the number shown. Whoever reaches the kitchen door first is the winner.

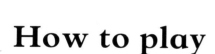

One, two, three, four
Mary at the kitchen door.
Five, six, seven, eight
Eating cherries off a plate.

Soldier

Sailor

Rich man

Queen

Poor man

Thief

Beggar man

Where Do Animals  Live?

In the snow, polar bear

In the fields, hare

In the forest, moose

In the sky,
dragonfly

In the woods, racoon

In the jungle, tiger

In the river, hippopotamus

In the desert, camel

In the pond, frog

On the plains, zebra

In a cave, bat

And what's this I see?
A head and a tail
In the deep blue ocean
An enormous WHALE!

Who Lives Here?

a palace for a princess

a den for a robber

a spacehouse for an astronaut

a cave for a monster

a ship for a pirate

The Story of the House

Once upon a time, a pig with a curly tail grew tired of living in his sty.

"I think," he said to his friend, the sheep, "I shall build myself a house."

"Good idea," said Sheep.

"On a hill," said Pig.

"Oooh," said Sheep, "can I come, too?"

"Well," said Pig, "what can you do to help?"

Sheep thought and then, "I can pull the logs to build the walls," he said.

"Come on, then," said Pig.

So the two of them, Pig and Sheep, went off together, and on the road they met a goose.

"Good morning, Pig," said Goose. "Good morning, Sheep. Where are you two going?"

"We're going to build a house," said Pig.

"On a hill," said Sheep.

"Oooh," said Goose, "can I come, too?"

"Well," said Pig, "what can you do to help?"

Goose thought and then "I can collect moss with my sharp beak," she said, "and I can stuff it into the cracks of the logs. That will keep out the wind and the rain."

"Come on, then," said Pig.

on the Hill

So the three of them, Pig, Sheep, and Goose, went off together, and on the way they met a rabbit.

"Good morning, Pig," said Rabbit. "And good morning, Sheep and Goose. Where are you three going?"

"We're going to build a house," said Pig.

"On a hill," said Sheep.

"With logs and moss," said Goose.

"Oooh," said Rabbit. "Can I come, too?"

"Well," said Pig, "what can you do to help?"

Rabbit thought and then, "I could dig the holes for the logs," he said.

"Come on, then," said Pig.

So the four of them, Pig, Sheep, Goose, and Rabbit, went off together, and on the way they met a rooster.

"Good morning Pig, Sheep, Goose, and Rabbit," he said. "Where are you four going?"

"We're going to build a house," said Pig.

"On a hill," said Sheep.

"With logs for walls," said Goose, "and moss to keep the wind out."

"And holes to keep the logs in place," said Rabbit.

"Oooh," said Rooster, "can I come, too?"

"Well," said Pig, "what can you do to help?"

Rooster thought and then, "I can crow very early each morning," he said, "and wake you up to begin your work."

"Come on, then," said Pig.

So the five of them, Pig, Sheep, Goose, Rabbit, and Rooster, went off together. And soon they came to a hill.

"There," said Pig, "is where I shall build my house."

And they all set to work.

Pig sniffed out the logs with his big snout; Sheep pulled them up the hill with his strong legs; Goose dug up moss with her sharp beak and stuffed it into the cracks. And Rabbit dug holes for the posts.

And every morning, very early, Rooster crowed to wake them all up so they could begin their work.

The house grew and grew. The walls went up. The windows went in. The roof went on. They all sat back and looked at the house they had built on the hill.

Then Rooster flew up to the roof and crowed and crowed with delight.

"Cock-a-doodle-doo!
Just come and look, please do!
We've worked away with such a will,
To build this house upon the hill.
Don't you think we've built it well?
And now inside we mean to dwell!"

Then everyone who lived for miles around heard the Rooster's song and knew that the house on the hill was finished.

And when they looked toward the house, they saw lights in the windows and smoke rising from the chimney, and they knew that inside the house the five friends were sitting together in great happiness.

Building . . . Outside

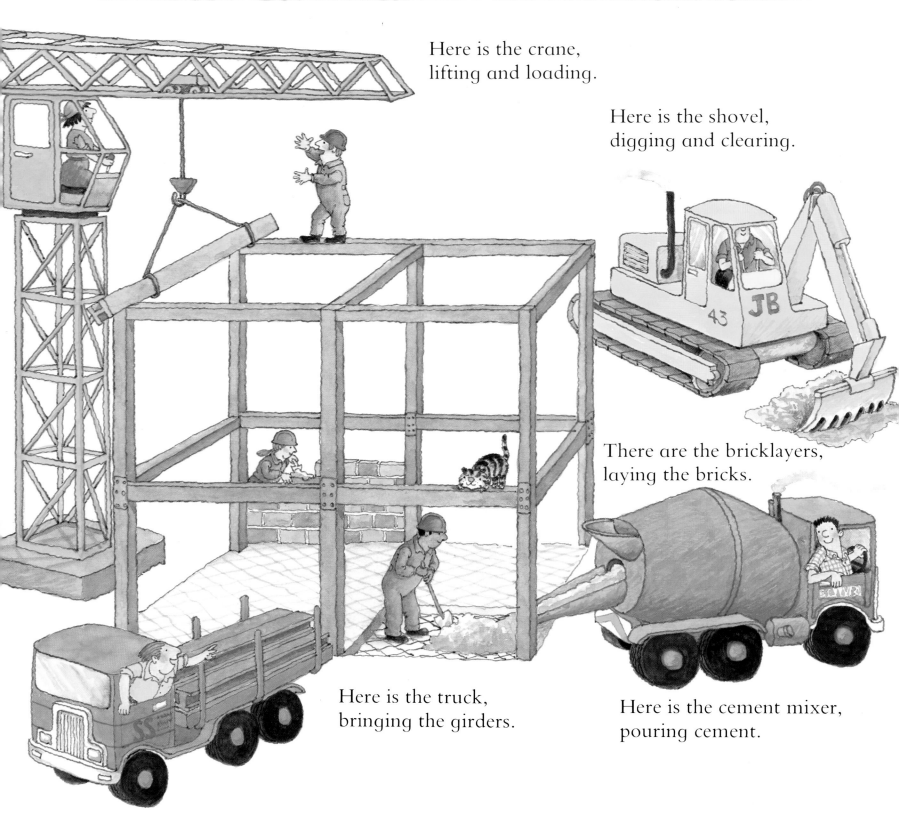

Here is the crane,
lifting and loading.

Here is the shovel,
digging and clearing.

There are the bricklayers,
laying the bricks.

Here is the truck,
bringing the girders.

Here is the cement mixer,
pouring cement.

. . . and Inside

Here are the plumbers, fitting in pipes
Here are the electricians, to put in the lights.
Here are the windows, and there are the doors.
Here are the carpenters, making the floors.

And here are the people living inside.

Where's the Yarn?

Granny wants to knit, but she can't find her ball of yarn.

Is it **under** the table? No.

Is it **over** the chair? No.

Is it **on top of** the books? No.

Is it **at the bottom of** the box? No.

Is it **in front** of the cat? No.

Is it **behind** the sofa? No.

Is it **in** the basket? No.

Is it **out of** the door . . .

Here It Is!

Braiding

Make braids by using different colored strands of thick yarn. Tie to the arm of a chair at the start.

Two thick braids can make a doll. Tie yarn tightly around as shown to make the head, waist, and legs, and sew on arms and features. (See the notes on stitches on page 90). Braids can also be stitched into mats or stuck on cards to make pictures.

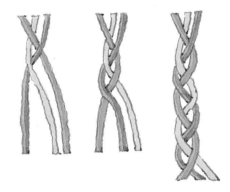

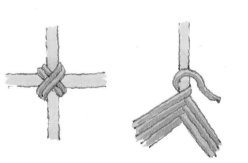

God's-eye weaving

Tie two sticks tightly together with one end of a ball of yarn. Hold the sticks in one hand and wind the yarn around them clockwise, and round and round each stick on the way. Change the color when you like. These make good Christmas decorations.

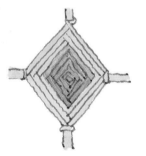

Woolly Things

Pompoms

Cut two circles of cardboard, and make a hole in the center of each. Wind yarn around the rings until they are full. Tie a piece of thread between the cards, cut the yarn, pull out the cards, then fluff out the pompom.

Slotted card weaving

Cut slots from a circle of cardboard and weave yarn around them. Pull up the sides as you go to make a bowl.

Threading

Practice threading and tying shoelaces. Draw a large boot or shoe on a piece of cardboard. Make holes for the eyelets and use a piece of yarn as the laces.

Baa, baa, black sheep,
Have you any wool?
Yes, sir, yes, sir,
Three bags full;
One for the master,
And one for the dame,
And one for the little boy
Who lives down the lane.

A sheep's haircut

Yarn comes from a sheep's coat. It is called a fleece. In spring, the fleece is cut off so that the sheep doesn't get too hot. It is cleaned, dyed, twisted into yarn, and then wound into balls.

Puppets

Do-it-yourself puppets are easy to make using scraps of material, yarn, string, buttons, and beads. (There are notes on knots and stitches on page 90.)

Wooden spoon puppet

Paint on a face, add yarn hair, and tie or glue on material as clothing.

Finger puppets

The simplest puppets are faces drawn on fingers with a felt-tip pen. The cutoff fingers of an old glove, little bags of felt, and even eggshells also make good finger puppets.

Matchbox puppet

Draw a face on the inside of an empty matchbox. Cut two holes in the front of the outer box and one at the back, and use your fingers as legs.

Scissor puppet

Cut out a cardboard figure about 5 inches high. Make two holes for your fingers as the legs.

Dance, Thumbkin, dance;
Dance, ye merry men, every one;
But Thumbkin, he can dance alone.
Dance, Thumbkin, dance.

Paper-bag puppet

Draw a face on a paper bag. Twist the corners to make ears.

Sock puppet

Paint a face or sew features on an old sock. Stitch both sides of the place where your fingers make the mouth to hold the shape.

Tube puppet

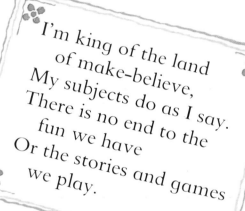

Paint a face on a cardboard tube. Glue some material around the bottom to hide your hand, and paint or glue on features and hair.

Witch puppet

Tie a handkerchief around your wrist. Paint eyes between your first and second fingers.

I'm king of the land of make-believe,
My subjects do as I say.
There is no end to the fun we have
Or the stories and games we play.

Make a stage

You can use the top of a table as a simple stage or make a more elaborate theater from a large cardboard box. Material looped on each side makes curtains. Paint a scene on the back of the box. Change the sets by painting other scenes on squares of cardboard attached to sticks hung over the sides of the box. Glue puppets on sticks, and lower them onto the stage.

Masks

All these masks can be made from cardboard. Cut the pieces to the sizes shown, and glue or staple them together. Hold the mask up to decide where the eye holes should be, and cut them out. Paint on a face or use yarn, felt, or pipe cleaners to make features. Cut out ears of the appropriate shape and glue them on. Make a small hole on each side of the mask, and knot a piece of elastic through them to keep the mask on.

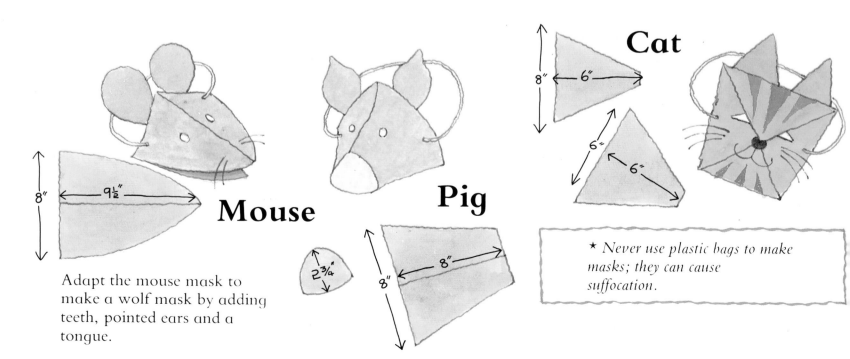

Cat

8" 6"

6" 6"

Mouse

8" 9½"

Adapt the mouse mask to make a wolf mask by adding teeth, pointed ears and a tongue.

Pig

2¾"

8" 8"

★ *Never use plastic bags to make masks; they can cause suffocation.*

and Hats

Witch's hat

Cut out a ring of cardboard to fit the child's head. Make a cone and cut slits around the bottom. Slip the ring over the cone and turn up the slits. Anchor them with tape or glue, and decorate the hat with foil or metallic paper.

Crown

Measure a strip of cardboard around the child's head, and cut it the right length. Cut triangles from the top, and decorate with foil, candy wrappers, or glitter.

Pirate's hat

Cut a piece of paper about 7 inches square. Fold it in half; then fold two equal triangles down from the folded edge. Turn up the strip of paper at the bottom; then turn the hat over and do the same on the other side. Paint on a skull and crossbones.

Clown's hat

Make several brightly colored pompoms (see page 59). Glue them to a cardboard cone or an old stocking cap. Glue some colored yarn around the inside to make a clown's wig.

People

Builder **Farmer** **Teacher** **Shoemaker**

Paper dolls

Make your own line of people by folding a piece of paper into pleats. Draw a figure on the front, making sure the arms and legs reach the folds. Cut around it, open out, and color in.

London's burning, London's burning,
Fetch the engines, fetch the engines.
Fire! Fire! Fire! Fire!
Pour on water, pour on water.

Elsie Marley has grown so fine,
She won't get up to feed the swine.
She lies in bed till eight or nine,
Lazy Elsie Marley.

Cobbler, cobbler, mend my shoe,
Get it done by half past two.
Stitch it up, and stitch it down,
Then I'll give you half a crown.

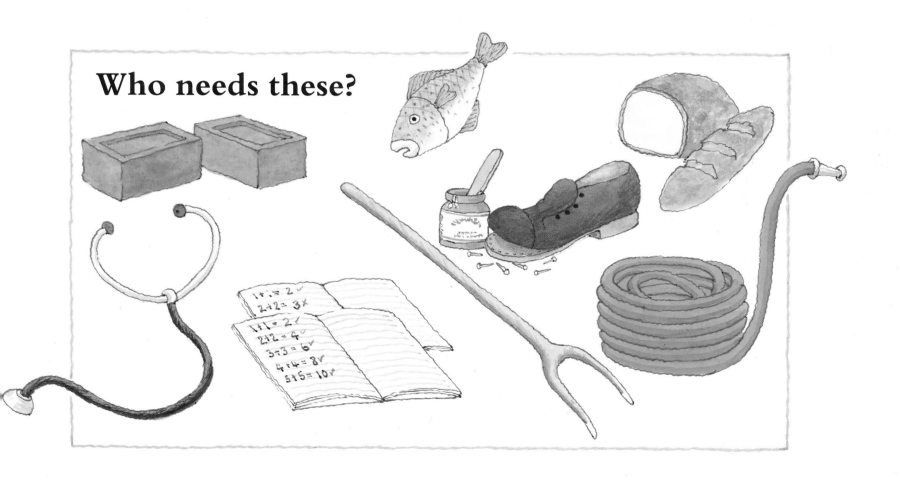

Baker **Doctor** **Fisherman** **Firefighter**

Who needs these?

The Story of the Town Mouse

Once upon a time, there lived a mouse – a stylish kind of fellow – whose home was in a very grand house in a town. Each day, he ate the best food, sipped the best wines, and at night slept in a warm little hole in the corner of the kitchen floor.

One day, however, he thought he'd like a change. "I could do with a vacation," he thought to himself. "I think I'll go and see my cousin, the country mouse, and get a breath of fresh air."

So he packed his bag, checked that his hole was clean and neat to come back to, and off he went.

His cousin was delighted to see him. "Come in, come in," he said. "Make yourself at home while I prepare a special meal for you."

And presently he invited his cousin to come to the table where he had laid a tablecloth with plates of bread and cheese, a few tomatoes, and a small leaf of lettuce.

The town mouse nibbled a little cheese. He took a mouthful or two of tomato and bread; he sipped clear, cool water. All the time, he was thinking rather longingly of the meal he might be enjoying in his own home – a pork chop perhaps, a portion of apple pie and ice cream, perhaps a glass of orange juice. But he quickly put such thoughts aside as being ungrateful, because he knew the country mouse was giving him the best food he could find.

"And now," said the country mouse, "you must be tired

and the Country Mouse

after your journey. Let me show you my guest hole."

And he led him to a small, scooped-out hole in the bank of a cornfield. Once again, the town mouse thought of his own warm nest, of the delicious smells of food which – all night long – tickled his nose and gave him such pleasant dreams, but, once again, he knew his cousin was giving him the best care he could, so he thanked him politely and settled down for the night.

But he could not sleep.

At first, it was too quiet. There were no sounds of traffic outside the door; there were no bursts of conversation from other rooms; there were no footsteps, no distant music like he could always hear in his own home when the sounds drifted down from upstairs rooms.

He tossed and turned.

Then he began to hear noises. He heard little scrabblings and scratchings as small night creatures came out of their homes and went about their business in the surrounding fields. And then – he shivered with fear at the sound – he heard the great whooping cry of an owl: "Too-wit! Too-woo!"

And no sooner had he closed his eyes than, "Breakfast!" called his cousin. "Time to get up!" And there on the breakfast table were a few grains of corn and barley, a glass of water, and – nothing else.

How, the town mouse wondered, when he had been so welcomed, could he tell his cousin that he wanted to go home? At last, he thought of what to say.

"Dear cousin," he said, "you have made me so welcome that I should like you to come back and stay with me for a few days. It is very quiet here, and I think perhaps you would like to see a little of town life?"

"Delighted," said the country mouse. That night they went off together, and by dawn they were safely inside the town house kitchen.

"Aha!" said the town mouse, rubbing his paws together with delight. "I see there was a party here last night! We have some roast beef, some special ice cream, a few cheeses . . . come and help yourself."

The country mouse gave a squeak of amazement at the sight of such rich food.

But just as they had begun their feast, Crash! Bang! the kitchen door burst open, and in came the cook in a great hurry. "Now, where's the bacon?" she muttered. "Where are those eggs?" And she rattled and clattered among the shelves of the pantry until the country mouse, who was crouched in fear behind a great pitcher of milk, thought he would die of fright.

When the cook had gone, the town mouse – not at all worried – popped out from behind a very large ham, saying cheerfully "All safe now! Come on out, my dear!"

But every time they began to eat, the same thing happened. Crash! Bang! would go the door, and in would come someone looking for food, or plates, or a skillet. There was never a moment's peace.

By nighttime, the country mouse was shaking like jelly. "Oh, it gets better at night," the town mouse assured him. "That's when we have really big feasts in this house. And the food they leave! You won't believe your eyes."

"I d . . . d . . . don't think I'll be here to see it!" said the country mouse. "I know my food is plain and simple; I know the country life is too quiet for an educated chap like you, but it suits me. And even though the food here is delicious, I never get the chance to eat it!" And a great tear rolled sadly down one cheek.

"Oh, please," said the town mouse, "don't be upset! I know how it is. Your life suits you, but it doesn't suit me. This life suits me, but it doesn't suit you – now where's the harm in that? We are both happy where we are, and, after all, we can always visit each other from time to time, can't we? It's so much better to live in the way each of us finds most comfortable."

"Ye . . . es," agreed the country mouse. "Can I go now?"

So the town mouse packed a small picnic basket for his cousin. In it he put a helping of salmon, a slice of roast beef, a little sausage, and a few strawberries. "There," he said. "You'll be back home for breakfast! Goodbye, cousin, we'll see each other again soon."

And back he went to his kitchen and his rich food, where he never noticed all the interruptions and the noise, because he had grown so used to them.

And scurrying along by the hedge, crossing fields, the country mouse was making his way back to his quiet little home. Around him, he could hear the scrabblings and scratchings of small night creatures looking for food. He heard the great whooping cry of the owl "Too-wit! Too-woo!" but these were the noises he was used to, and they didn't worry him at all.

And at last he came to his own home in the scooped-out bank of the cornfield, and, with a sigh of satisfaction, he said to himself, "It's best to stay in the place that suits you best."

So he unpacked his picnic and in the peace of the early morning he ate a hearty breakfast of salmon and strawberries. "The roast beef and sausage I'll save for supper," he said to himself and then, feeling very drowsy after his journey and his large breakfast, he curled himself into a ball and fell fast asleep. With not a sound to disturb him.

A, My Name Is Alice

A, my name is Alice and I sell airplanes

B, my name is Billy and I sell boats

C, my name is Cleo and I sell canaries

D, my name is Danny and I sell dragons

E, my name is Emma and I sell elephants

F, my name is Freddy and I sell flowers

G, my name is Gomez and I sell giraffes

H, my name is Hannah and I sell helicopters

I, my name is Izzy and I sell invitations

J, my name is Jake and I sell jeans

K, my name is Katie and I sell kangaroos

L, my name is Lloyd and I sell lions

a b c d e f g h i j k l m n o p q r s t u v w x y z

M, my name is Malik and I sell masks

N, my name is Nancy and I sell nuts

O, my name is Oscar and I sell oranges

P, my name is Polly and I sell parrots

Q, my name is Quentin and I sell quarters of cake

R, my name is Richard and I sell ribbons

S, my name is Sarah and I sell snakes

T, my name is Tariq and I sell trains

U, my name is Umberto and I sell uniforms

V, my name is Valerie and I sell violins

W, my name is Walter and I sell watermelons

And we three, Xavier, Yim-Mai, and Zack, do the shopping!

Letters, Words,

Writing letters, and making cards, and sending them to friends and relatives, is an enjoyable way to introduce letters and words. There are notes on writing on page 91.

Window card

Cut out a rectangle of paper or thin cardboard. Fold it in half, and cut a square out of the front. Draw a picture on the inside that can be seen through the window.

Peek-a-boo card

Cut out a rectangle of paper or thin cardboard. Fold it in half and open out. Cut off the top left side. Close the card and lightly mark the top of the cut side. Draw a picture on the inside, making sure that only part of it peeps over the top of the line. Erase the pencil mark.

Zigzag card

Fold a strip of paper into a zigzag. Draw on one side and write the message on the pages.

Word games

Word games can be simple, like "I spy," or complicated like the alphabet game below.

ALPHABET GAME

The first person says that they are taking a trip to a place beginning with A. The next player repeats the sentence and adds an object they are taking with them beginning with B, and so on through the alphabet.

I took a trip to Alaska.

I took a trip to Alaska with a boat.

 # and Scrapbooks

Make your own scrapbooks from thick paper sewn or stapled down the middle. Let the child decide what will go in it – tickets, photos, drawings – and write under each one where it came from or what it reminds you both of.

Or make a scrapbook about a specific topic like color, the alphabet, or animals. Draw or cut out pictures of the objects you choose, and write the name underneath. Encourage the child to draw or find the objects, and put them into groups: a page for yellow objects, or objects beginning with A, for example.

red

yarn

Sarah's dress

I found this feather

my ball

Sand from the beach

train to the zoo

giraffe

my thumb print

I took a trip to Alaska with a boat and a canary.

I took a trip to Alaska with a boat, a canary, and a dragon.

I took a trip to Alaska with a boat, a canary, a dragon, and an elephant.

Small,

Guess the opposites from the pictures.

If it is not small,
then it is . . .

If it is not quick,
then it is . . .

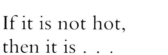

If it is not tall,
then it is . . .

If it is not wet,
then it is . . .

If it is not hot,
then it is . . .

If it is not fat,
then it is . . .

If it is not new, then it is . . .

Sing a song of sizes
Who will win the prizes?
All our clothes are mixed up.
Won't you help us? Do!

Big,

If it is not smooth,
then it is . . .

If it is not noisy,
then it is . . .

If it is not heavy,
then it is . . .

If it is not full,
then it is . . .

If it is not day,
then it is . . .

If it is not dirty,
then it is . . .

If it is not tiny, then it is . . .
(Turn over for a BIG surprise!)

Which is the quickest way to go?
Which is much, much too slow?

HUGE!

Dinosaurs lived on earth millions
of years ago. Most of them were huge – like this
Stegosaurus (STEG-oh-SAW-rus) which
grew up to 18 feet long and could weigh
2 or 3 tons. But the biggest dinosaur of
all – Ultrasaurus – could grow
up to 100 feet long and weigh as much
as 30 tons. That's as long as two buses
and as heavy as 25 elephants!

Sneezy, Freezy,

Whether the weather be nice, or whether the weather be not,

Showery
Flowery
Bowery

SPRING

Hoppy
Croppy
Poppy

SUMMER

We'll weather the weather, whatever the weather,

Wheezy
Sneezy
Breezy

FALL

Slippy
Drippy
Nippy

WINTER

Whether we like it or not!

Flowery, Showery

Watch the weather as the seasons change around you. Talk about the different aspects of weather – the clothes you need to wear and what happens to plants and animals, for example.

Shadow stick

Make your own sundial with an upright stick. Mark where the shadow falls at 9, 12, 3, and 6 o'clock.

Who has seen the wind?
Neither I nor you:
But when the leaves hang
    trembling,
The wind is passing through.
Christina Rossetti

I have a little shadow
That goes in and out
    with me
And what can be the
    use of him
Is more than I can see.
R. L. Stevenson

Raindrop race

Each person chooses a raindrop at the top of a window. The person whose drop reaches the bottom of the pane first is the winner.

Bird cake

In winter, combine breadcrumbs, nuts, and grated cheese with melted shortening in a bowl. When the "cake" hardens place it safely outside.

Rain on the green grass,
Rain on the trees.
Rain on the rooftops,
But not on me.

In the bleak midwinter,
Frosty made wind moan.
Earth stood hard as iron,
Water like a stone.
Christina Rossetti

What's the Time?

What happens first?

Decide which picture should come first, then second, third, and last.

How to make a clock

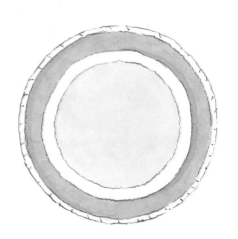
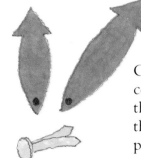

Cut two hands from cardboard. Attach them with a brad in the center of a paper plate. Draw on the numbers and a face, and add a loop of ribbon or string to hang the clock up.

Make a Hickory Dickory clock

Hickory Dickory Dock,
The mouse ran up
the clock.
The clock struck one,
The mouse ran down,
Hickory Dickory Dock.

Cut a slit 2 inches long above the 6 of the clock. Trace the mouse opposite on cardboard and color it. Thread a ribbon through the slit, and glue on the mouse and 2 circles of cardboard. Pull the ribbon to watch the mouse run up the clock!

The Story of the Hare

Once upon a time, a hare sat looking at a tortoise who was chewing a lettuce leaf.

"You eat slowly," he said, "and you walk slowly. Don't you get tired of always being so slow?"

"Nope," said the tortoise.

"Now I'm very fast," continued the hare. "I can run like the wind. I could run all around this field and back again before you've finished chewing that leaf. Shall I try?"

"Yep," said the tortoise.

Off set the hare . . . *whee . . . whizz* . . . down the field, around the corners . . . *puff, pant, pant, pant*; and he screeched to a halt just as the last mouthful was disappearing down the tortoise's throat.

"See what I mean?" he asked.

"Yep," said the tortoise.

"Let's have a race," said the hare. "Of course I'll win, but let's see how far I can run. We'll go right around the field and back here. Are you ready?

"Yep," said the tortoise.

On your mark, get set, go – and off they went.

The hare raced. The tortoise plodded. *Whee . . . Whizz* . . . the hare looked behind him. The tortoise wasn't even in sight.

"Hmm," thought Hare. "I'll just have a snack of those delicious-looking leaves over there. Plenty of time. Old Plod will never catch me up."

The leaves were delicious. The hare ate and ate. He ate so much his middle looked like a balloon.

"Whew!" he said. He looked around. The tortoise was *just* in sight . . . plod, plod, plod.

and the Tortoise

So off he raced. Heels in the air, ears flattened. *Whee . . . whizz . . .* screeching around the corner. Then he stopped and looked behind.

No sign of old Plod.

"Oh, well," thought Hare. "I'm nearly home again. There's plenty of time for a rest – and I do feel rather full!"

So down he lay in the shade of some bushes, and within seconds he was fast asleep.

He slept and he slept. At last, he woke. He stretched himself and yawned. "I suppose I'd better finish this race," he thought. "Though there's no need to hurry – I'm nearly home."

So he got to his feet and began to saunter the last few yards. He turned the last corner. And what did he see?

Tortoise chewing a lettuce leaf.

"W . . . wh . . . what's happened?" he stammered. 'H . . . how did you get here? Did you really go all around the field?"

"Yep," said the tortoise.

"You didn't cheat?"

"Nope."

"But . . . but . . . I looked back when I was having a snack . . . you weren't anywhere near."

"Nope."

"And when I woke up from my nap you were nowhere in sight!"

"Nope."

"Then how did you get here first?" asked Hare.

"Just kept plodding," said Plod. "Didn't stop for a snack; didn't stop for a nap. Just plodded." And he finished the last mouthful of lettuce leaf.

Growing Up

An interest in growing up can be an introduction to a sense of history, especially if you relate it to your own family through stories and old photographs. Make a family tree using stick figure drawings or photos if you have them. Begin as far back as you can, and write in the names of all the family members you know.

Arthur Mouse's family tree

Mom's Grandparents
My Great-Grandparents

Albert Albertine

Dad's Grandparents
My Great-Grandparents

Manuel Manuela

Mom's Parents
My Grandparents

Gramps Granny

Mom's Uncle
My Great Uncle

Uncle David

Dad's Aunt
My Great Aunt

Aunt Selina

Dad's Parents
My Grandparents

Nanna Grandad

My Uncle My Aunt
Mom's sister

Uncle Fred Aunt Mary

My Parents

Mom Dad

Dad's brother My Aunt
My Uncle

Uncle James Aunt Lucy

My Cousins

Jack   Ann   Frances

ME!   My   My
       Brother Sister

Arthur   Fred   Sue

My Cousin

Jim

Let your child see how he or she is growing as time passes by marking height on a wall or door frame once or twice each year. Or make a decorative hanging from a long strip of cardboard or fabric.

Last year's shoes won't fit my feet,
Nor last year's hat my head.
Soon I'll have no clothes to wear
I'll have to stay in bed!
But when I think about it hard,
I think I really know
Like kittens, chicks and even seeds,
All children have to grow!

Carolyn July.

Carolyn Nov.

Gemma July.

Gemma Nov.

Tape pieces of paper together to make a long scroll. Divide it into weeks, and write down important events which have happened or which you are looking forward to. Draw pictures, too.

Swimming Lesson

Moved house

Gemma's birthday

Cat had Kittens

Christmas

Times Around the Day

7 o'clock

8 o'clock

9 o'clock

10 o'clock

11 o'clock

12 o'clock

1 o'clock

2 o'clock

3 o'clock

4 o'clock

5 o'clock

6 o'clock

. . . and Night

7 o'clock

8 o'clock

9 o'clock

10 o'clock

11 o'clock

12 o'clock

1 o'clock

2 o'clock

3 o'clock

4 o'clock

5 o'clock

6 o'clock

Time To Sleep

Oh! hush thee, my baby, the night is behind us,
    And black are the waters that sparkled so green.
The moon o'er the combers, looks downward to find us,
    At rest in the hollows that rustle between.
Where billow meets billow, then soft be thy pillow;
    Ah, weary wee flipperling, curl at thy ease.
The storm shall not wake thee,
    Nor shark overtake thee,
Asleep in the arms of the
    Slow-swinging seas.

Rudyard Kipling

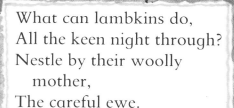

What can lambkins do,
All the keen night through?
Nestle by their woolly
    mother,
The careful ewe.

What can nestlings do,
In the nightly dew?
Sleep beneath their
mother's wing,
Till day breaks anew.

If in field or tree,
There might only be,
Such a warm soft sleeping
    place,
Found for me!

Christina Rossetti

Hush-a-bye baby
In the tree top.
When the wind blows,
The cradle will rock;

When the bough breaks,
The cradle will fall;
Down will come baby,
Cradle and all.

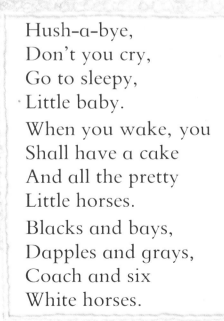

Hush-a-bye,
Don't you cry,
Go to sleepy,
Little baby.

When you wake, you
Shall have a cake
And all the pretty
Little horses.

Blacks and bays,
Dapples and grays,
Coach and six
White horses.

Useful Information

Stitches

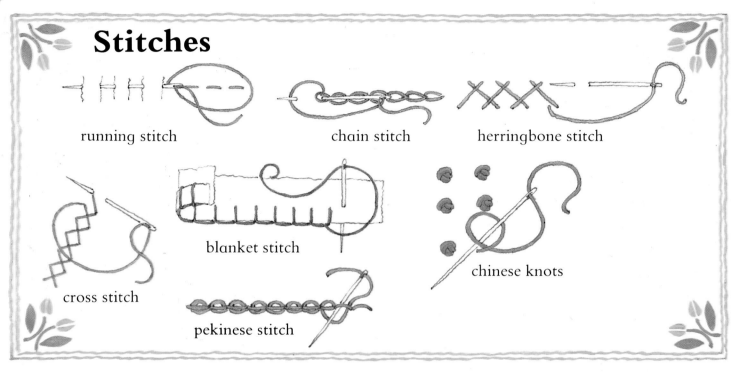

running stitch   chain stitch   herringbone stitch

blanket stitch

cross stitch

pekinese stitch

chinese knots

Knots

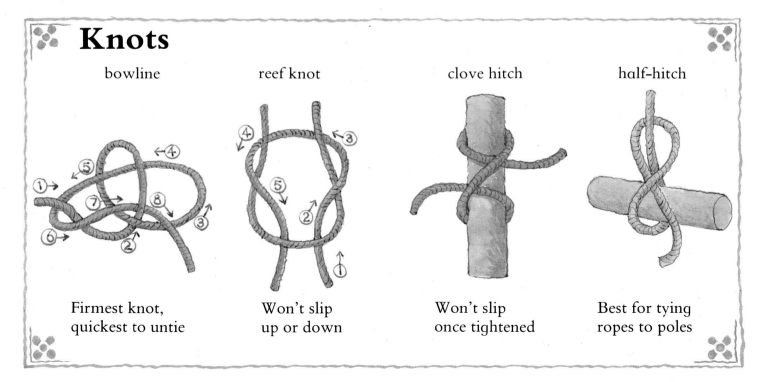

bowline   reef knot   clove hitch   half-hitch

Firmest knot, quickest to untie

Won't slip up or down

Won't slip once tightened

Best for tying ropes to poles

Preparing to read and write

Early reading involves memory, guesswork, and lots of help from pictures. Children only learn to recognize words out of context very slowly. They often learn words by recognizing the initial letter and letter sound.

Patterns like these will help a child when he or she begins to form letters. Try drawing them with dotted lines so that the child can trace over them or try to join the dots.

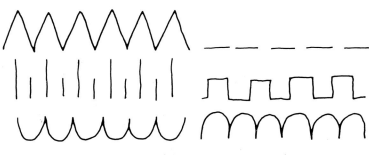

This is how a child should hold a pencil. The index finger should be nearly straight and the hold relaxed. A young child will invariably grip too tightly, but will loosen up as confidence and dexterity increase.

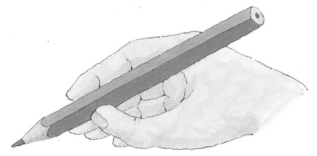

Always begin by teaching a child to form lower-case letters. The right place to start each letter is shown by the heavy dots. Move the pencil in the direction of the arrows. Don't force a child, or make it into a "lesson." A child who sees his parents enjoying books will want to learn to read and write.

Useful Information
Recipes

Paste

1 cup flour or cornstarch
1 cup cold water
1 cup boiling water
Dissolve the flour in the
cold water. Add the
boiling water, and stir
quickly to reduce lumps.

Finger paint

1 cup cornstarch or flour
1 cup cold water
3 cups boiling water
Powder paint or food coloring
Make the paste as above, then
mix in the coloring. Soap
powder mixed with very hot
water and food coloring also
makes good finger paint.

Bubbles

1 cup liquid detergent
2 cups water
Mix together well. A ¼ tsp
of glycerine or cooking
oil added to the mixture
will make the bubbles
stronger.

Playdough

Mix together 2 cups flour, 1 cup salt, 1 tbsp. oil,
a little food coloring, and 1 cup water. Knead well.
The dough will dry out when exposed to air, but
will keep for two or three weeks in an airtight
container.

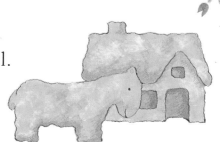

Modeling dough you can eat

Cream together 6 ounces of butter and 8 ounces of sugar. Add an egg
and beat well. Mix in 2½ cups flour. Add flavoring and coloring. This
dough needs to be baked at 350° for 15 minutes if models are ½ inch
thick or less; thicker shapes will need longer in the oven.

Index

HD